The Piano

by **William Miller**

illustrated by **Susan Keeter**

LEE & LOW BOOKS INC. • NEW YORK

Text copyright © 2000 by William Miller
Illustrations copyright © 2000 by Susan Keeter

Printed in Hong Kong by South China Printing Co. (1988) Ltd.

Book design by Tania Garcia
Book production by The Kids at Our House

The text is set in Sabon
The illustrations are rendered in oil paint

10 9 8 7 6 5 4 3 2
First Edition

Library of Congress Cataloging-in-Publication Data

Miller, William.
      The piano / by William Miller ; illustrated by Susan Keeter. —
1st ed.
            p.   cm.
      Summary: A young black girl's love of music leads her to a job
in the home of an older white woman who not only teaches her to
play the piano but also about caring for others.
      ISBN 1-880000-98-9
      [1. Piano Fiction. 2. Old age Fiction. 3. Afro-Americans
Fiction.] I. Keeter, Susan, ill. II. Title.
PZ7.M63915Pi   2000
[E]—dc21   99-38004
                                                        CIP

For Aunt Dot and Uncle Gene, the best people,
the best parents in the world —W.M.

To Bernice "Granny" Nunn, the good friend and shepherd of
many children, and to Cecil A. Tankersley, my grandfather-in-law,
who shared his memories of life in southern Georgia —S.K.

Tia loved music. The sound of a blues guitar or a child singing made her feel wonderful inside. When she heard music, she forgot where she lived, how old she was, and where she went to school.

Tia spent her days searching for music. Her mother and brothers worked in the cotton mill, so she was free to roam the summer streets.

One morning, Tia crossed the railroad tracks to the white section of town. She wandered down the wide streets listening, searching. She had never done this before, but she was hungry for new sounds, different music.

Tia was on her way back home when she first heard the music. The melody drifted lazily across the wide, green lawn. It made Tia think of castles, mountains, and deep new snow. The music took her far away from the hot, dry town.

"You come about the job?" A boy in overalls tapped Tia on the shoulder.

"What job?" Tia asked, her mind filled with music, fields of bright snow.

"The maid's job," replied the boy. "Miss Hartwell was hoping for somebody older, but I guess you'll do." He motioned for Tia to follow him. "Name's Johnny," he added.

Tia didn't want a job, least of all maid's work, but she did want to hear more of the music.

"Miss Hartwell," Johnny called out. An elderly white woman walked into the kitchen. Even though it was morning, she was dressed like she was going to a party.

"Can you clean floors?" Miss Hartwell asked. Tia nodded without thinking. The music that had drawn her to the house was still playing in the next room.

"My windows get mighty dirty," Miss Hartwell said. "Are you sure a girl your age can handle that?"

Once again, Tia nodded without thinking. She was too busy listening to the beautiful music.

"All right," Miss Hartwell sighed. "We'll give you a try."

Johnny showed Tia where the mops
and brushes were and Tia began to clean the
kitchen floor. Her back ached and her fingers
hurt, but the music took her mind off the work.
After the floor was cleaned, Tia peeked through the
door that separated the kitchen from the parlor. She saw
Miss Hartwell listening to a record player, her eyes closed.
Tia saw something else, too. In the corner, by the record
player, was a piano, bigger than any she had ever seen. The black
wood shone brighter than a new pair of Sunday shoes.

That afternoon, when Miss Hartwell was taking a nap, Tia tiptoed over to the piano. She pressed the keys as if they were made of glass, as if they would break beneath her fingers. Relaxing, she pressed harder, faster, making sounds that were little more than beautiful noise.

"Do you like my piano?" Miss Hartwell asked.

"Oh!" said Tia, jumping up. "I'm sorry. I only wanted to . . ."

"It's all right," Miss Hartwell said. She sat down on the bench and patted the seat beside her.

"You must hold your fingers above the keys and play softly."
Miss Hartwell tried to demonstrate, but her hands were stiff
with age. Tia saw the pain in her eyes when she tried to play.

"I better get back to work now," Tia said. She was afraid
Miss Hartwell was going to cry.

"All right," Miss Hartwell said softly.

In the days that followed, Tia went back to the house. She met Johnny at the gate and followed him inside.

As soon as Miss Hartwell lay down for her nap, Tia went to the piano. She did as Miss Hartwell had said, curving her fingers above the keys, playing them lightly. She tried to find those keys that fit the sounds of the music that poured out of the record player. Sometimes she was certain she had found a note or two that matched, and she played them over and over. But Tia knew she would never learn to play without a real teacher.

One afternoon, as Miss Hartwell was going upstairs, Tia stopped her.

"Miss Hartwell," Tia said quietly. "Will you teach me to play the piano? I could pay you my wages. I'll work just for the lessons."

Miss Hartwell smiled sadly. "These hands don't play very well anymore."

"But you could talk me through the music — tell me what to do, like the first day."

"All right, Tia," Miss Hartwell said. "But I certainly won't have you paying me. We'll see how much you can learn."

Tia watched carefully as Miss Hartwell taught her notes, a simple scale. Miss Hartwell winced in pain, but the more she played, the less the pain seemed to bother her.

When Tia learned the notes of the scale and played them swiftly, Miss Hartwell nodded her approval. Tia wanted to play the same scale again, but Miss Hartwell insisted she begin a new one.

"There is so much to learn," Miss Hartwell said. "So much."

At the end of the lesson, Tia could see how badly Miss Hartwell's hands were hurting her.

"Please wait here, Miss Hartwell," Tia said and disappeared into the kitchen. She came back with a bowl of warm water, a washcloth, and a shaker of salt.

"What are you doing, girl?" Miss Hartwell asked as Tia poured salt into the bowl.

Tia dipped the washcloth into the warm, salty water and gently rubbed Miss Hartwell's swollen hands.

"Tia, don't," Miss Hartwell said, sounding embarrassed.

"It's okay," Tia said. "I do this for my mama when she comes home from the mill. She taught me about the salt."

"It feels good," Miss Hartwell said in a low voice. "The warm water feels good."

Two weeks later, Johnny was waiting for Tia outside the gate.

"I just came to say goodbye," Johnny said. "I got me a better job down the street. It pays five cents more."

"But what about Miss Hartwell?" Tia asked. "Who's going to chop the firewood and light the stove?"

"Don't look at me," Johnny said. "All white people's money is the same. I don't care which ones I get it from."

Johnny tipped his hat. "Good luck with the old lady. Maybe you'll get a better job, too."

Tia didn't care about a better job. All she cared about was the piano, making the music Miss Hartwell taught her to play.

Tia closed the gate behind her and hurried to the woodpile. Raising the ax high above her head, Tia struck the logs until there was enough kindling. She carried the sticks inside and knelt before the stove. The flames made her sweat and the wash pot was almost too heavy to lift.

"Where's Johnny?" Miss Hartwell asked when she came into the kitchen. Tia told her about Johnny's new job, but not the part about white people's money.

"I can take care of the house," Tia insisted. "We don't need Johnny. I can do his chores and mine. Then we can play the piano."

"You're going to hurt yourself," Miss Hartwell said. "I'll hire someone else . . ."

"But please, just for today, I'll do the work," Tia pleaded.

Tia was determined, and nothing Miss Hartwell said could stop her.

When the time came for her lesson, Tia was exhausted. Her feet ached and sharp pains shot through her small hands. She sat at the piano, touching the keys with numb fingertips.

"Don't you move from there," Miss Hartwell said firmly. She stood up slowly, stiffly, and went into the kitchen. She came back with a bowl of warm water, a washcloth, and a shaker of salt.

"A friend of mine taught me this trick," Miss Hartwell said, gently rubbing Tia's hands with the warm cloth.

Tia tried to pull her hands back, but Miss Hartwell wouldn't let her.

"If you're going to be a great piano player, you have to take care of these fingers," Miss Hartwell told Tia. "Now let's try that piece we started yesterday."

Her fingers still hurt, but Tia soon forgot the pain. Once more she thought of castles, mountains, and snow falling through winter trees. Once more she left the hot, dry town behind her.

This time, Miss Hartwell went with her.